Little Rabbit couldn't sleep

For Steph
B.S.

For Oliver and Joshua
S.A.

First published in 2009 by Meadowside Children's Books

This edition published in 2011 by Little Bee,
an imprint of Meadowside Children's Books, 185 Fleet Street, London EC4A 2HS
www.meadowsidebooks.com

Text © Beth Shoshan 2009
Illustrations © Sarah Arnold 2009
The rights of Beth Shoshan and Sarah Arnold to be identified
as the author and illustrator of this work have been asserted by
them in accordance with the Copyright, Designs and Patents Act, 1988

A CIP catalogue record for this book is available
from the British Library
Printed in China

10 9 8 7 6 5 4 3 2 1

Little Rabbit couldn't sleep

little bee

Little Rabbit
 couldn't sleep…

In the day,
the sun is there,
warm and bright.

But when night comes,
the sky hangs low,
dark and empty.

"If I fall asleep now, there'll be no one
watching over me," thought Little Rabbit.
"I'll just have to wait for the moon."

And so he did just that.

The trouble with being
so tired and sleepy,
was that he didn't know exactly
when the moon would come.

Little Rabbit
waited and waited.

More time passed and the moon still hadn't come.

He thought he had better ask someone how much longer he might have to wait.

"This is my first day, ever,"
said a small flower in the fields.
"Maybe I will have grown into a tree
by the time your moon comes."

That sounded like an awfully long time.

Little Rabbit thought he had better
ask someone else – just to be sure.

"Look deep into the water,"
shimmered a little lake nearby.
"Maybe your moon has fallen in
and can't get out."

That didn't sound like what he
wanted to hear.

Little Rabbit thought he had better
ask someone else – just to be sure.

"Why don't you walk with me?"
twisted a long and winding path.
"We can find out where I'm leading
and maybe your moon is at the other end!"

That sounded like it might
be a long way away.

Little Rabbit thought he had better ask
someone else – just to be sure.

"I've just blown in to these parts,"
breezed a wind that had picked up.
"Who knows? I might be a big, fierce storm
by the time your moon comes."

That didn't sound like something
he wanted to wait for.

Little Rabbit thought he had better
ask someone else – just to be sure.

"We can't see your moon yet,"
rumbled the great, rolling hills.
"And we can see far into
the distance from up here!"

That didn't sound very promising.

Little Rabbit began to think
that the moon might never come.
And he was getting awfully tired...

And then, from behind the hills,
carried by the wind
   along the twists of the path,
   reflected in the lake,
      and shining on the petals
      of the small flower…

...the most perfect moon
slid into the night sky.

But Little Rabbit
had fallen asleep,
dreaming of the moon that would
watch over him through the night.